Dear Mom, I

MW01092161

A collection of poems between a mother and her USMC recruit

By Andy Hefty

Introduction

The perspective of this collection of poems is primarily that of a mother and her male recruit at Marine Corps Recruit Depot, Parris Island, South Carolina. There will be some references to a father, a female recruit, and some different perspectives as well. That said, if your recruit or parental situation is different than what is outlined herein, please apply yours accordingly.

As a veteran of the Marine Corps, and also a father of a Marine, I have written these poems from the viewpoint of being involved on the inside and then being on the sidelines waiting for the occasional, sometimes elusive, letter. Knowing the anxiety that some face waiting to hear something – anything – about what is going on in the transition from a youngster to a man or woman ready to fight for our nation, I hope to have captured the heart and mindset of those anxious moments.

Some of the poems may seem a bit dark, while others are lighthearted, and the rest somewhere between. I've tried to reflect the reality of the time at Boot Camp as best as possible.

While this book is not yet complete, it should capture what everyone is feeling, thinking, and in some cases writing. I hope you find it a blessing as you await to hug your Marine for the first time since his or her departure.

And for those whose children have already earned that coveted title, this is for you as well. Let it be a reflection of all you have overcome and a way of encouraging others on this roller coaster journey.

God Bless You! Andy

To Armand

Glad to serve our
country.

Semper F.!

Andy "Bags" Hefty
Sgt   USMC
1982-90

Dedication

This book is dedicated to so many people, that it is hard to list them all. But here goes.

Jesus Christ. No introduction needed. But without His strength, without His love, I'd be lost.

My wife, Mary, and my 12 children. Their support and encouragement have meant the world to me. Without Mary's prodding me to write down so many of my thoughts, I probably never would have done it. Thank you, Dear. LuvU!!!

Lynn Hallman Hayes. Lynn is a volunteer who should be paid more than any high-priced athlete for the work that she puts in managing all the support pages on Facebook. Even though I had a good idea what my son Stephen was going through, it was Lynn's daily posts that kept my wife's sanity.

GySgt Dane Hayes (Lynn's son) & SSgt Lori Devine. Dane is a former drill instructor. He and Lori are active duty Marines who assisted me with technical advice. Since my knowledge of Boot Camp is from 1982, it was somewhat dated. Dane and Lori kept my information fresh.

Ben Hermann. Ben was my recruiter (at the time a GySgt, but I believe he retired a Master Sergeant). Growing up in a Navy family, I had originally planned to go to Orlando (then an active Navy Boot Camp). But Ben challenged me. I love a good challenge.

Jim "Pack" Barta, LtCol, USMC Retired. JJ Barta was my first commanding officer in the fleet. He was a hard-charging, lead-by-example Marine, fighter pilot, and leader. Everyone who served under his command would have followed him to storm the very gates of hell if he'd have simply suggested we pay the devil a visit. He had a unique way of motivating his troops that could never be duplicated.

Everyone here (and many others along life's journey) have inspired
me to strive for the very best in everything I do. And for that, I am
eternally grateful.

Dear Mom, Don't Worry

Dear Mom, I know
That you're worried sick
But I'm doing ok
In the sand ever thick

We're learning a lot
About Country and Corps
One thing is certain
Boot Camp isn't a bore

It's mind over matter
They tell us each day
It keeps our nerves
From starting to fray

There's strength in numbers
I've learned with each task
These men are my buddies
There's no need to ask

We're in this together
Come whatever there might
The harder the challenge
The stronger we fight

The days here are grueling
The DIs only frown
But I'm working to make proud
Everyone in our town

Knowing you're praying
For me every night
Gives me great comfort
To keep up the fight

So don't worry, Mom

I've got it together
Just want you to know
I love you forever

Going to MEPS

I never understood acronyms
Especially the military variety
But with this first exposure to them
I finally was hit with the sobriety

A poolee you have been
For almost a year
Training and learning
For the future now so near

And here is the day
Your official swearing in
I held back the tears
And fought off a grin

When the captain said to all
Raise your right hands
I couldn't help but wonder
About those faraway lands

The ones where you might go
And fight for us all
But before you do that
You have a task that is quite tall

The last day of your life
That you'll be fully at ease
In a few short hours
It'll be anything but a breeze

One more hug, maybe two
Before you board the van
We'll pray for you daily
Please write when you can

I promise I won't cry

My goodbyes I have spoken
Now that you're gone
That earlier promise I've broken

I'll be ok
Maybe some time tomorrow
Other mommas will help me
Get through my sorrow

Be strong and courageous
Keep your heart and eyes keen
I'll see you in a few months
A U. S. Marine

You've got this, recruit!

When we said our goodbyes
And you left far away
I held you so tight
Wanting you to stay

But to serve our great nation
You answered the call
So behind you we stand
Strong, proud, and tall

Times won't be easy
In fact they'll be tough
But what it takes to make it
You have more than enough

You've got this, Recruit
Get rough, big, and mean
We will see you soon
A United States Marine

On the way...

Dear Mom I know
Your life is about to get rough
But like my recruiter told me
I'm urging you to hang tough

After swearing in
And saying goodbye
I saw your eyes well up
And asked you not to cry

Though I know your heart
And you pledged not to weep
This is one promise
You don't have to keep

But don't worry
About what lies ahead
Boot Camp and the future
I neither fear nor dread

You raised me well
With a steady heart and strong mind
And in the next few weeks
Your composure you'll find

Until the day you hear from me
By letter in postal mail
Know that I left a part of my heart
To comfort your emotions so frail

So steady your heart, Mom
Stand tall and be strong
This roller coaster ride
Won't last very long

I'm ready now

To be among the best
And with this letter
Let me put your fears to rest

Next time I see you
I'll be strong and lean
In thirteen grueling weeks
A United States Marine

I got the call, but I'm a wreck

I got the call
At 10:30 tonight
But now I can't sleep
My life is now a fright

He was shouting
Over dozens of recruits
They hadn't even issued
His uniforms and boots

He said he was safe
And of that I'm sure
His voice rang true
A but hoarse, but still pure

And now starts the worry
Concern, dread, and fear
I need to talk to a friend
Someone I trust and hold dear

Let me go online
To vent to the other mothers
They know what to do
They help out like they're brothers

"You got this" dear mom
Said several at once
They helped calm me down
I really love this bunch

Under the leadership
Of Lynn Hallman Hayes
This group can lend comfort
With one simple phrase

No doubt I'll be spending

Much of my spare time
With this group of parents
To prevent an idle mind

What are they doing?
Let me look at the schedule
This info is vital
For my sanity, essential

Thank you to all
Recruit and Marine mothers
Your support in this tough spot
Is like no other

Lord help me and guide me
Keep me from weeping
I feel better now
I'm going to try sleeping

Hang up and move it!

"Hang up and move it!"
They shouted in my ears
I've never been screamed at
Like this in all my years

We just left the footprint
On that famous, sacred street
At full attention
We landed our feet

And now beginning processing,
They took all our stuff
I never imagined
The first day would be this rough

I'm hungry and tired
Sweaty and afraid
My voice growing hoarse
Has already decayed

Keep shouting and moving
Obey every command
They're prepping you
To defend our great land

Now off to get uniforms
Equipment and gear
Just do what they say
Without any fear

I tremble inside
My heart is a flutter
Keep shouting loudly
Don't ever mutter

Starting this journey

Never look back
But when, Drill Instructor
Will we hit the rack?

My recruiter prepared me
My mother is praying
Any more screaming
And we will sound like we're braying

Quickest shower on record
Then into uniform
Now into the next building
Before the thunderstorm

So much has happened
In the last couple hours
Is that the sun coming up?
Keep moving, don't cower

I've got this, Mom
Don't stalk the mailman
I'll write at first chance
Just as soon as I can

Still no word

Today is the day
When they meet their DI
On San Diego
Or on the island, PI

I've heard nothing from him
Since that dreadful first call
I am not the only one
Who wants to sit here and bawl

What's going on?
What are they thinking?
Are their hearts like mine
Heavy and fast-sinking?

The Drill Instructor oath
Belted loudly and strong
Assures our recruits
That their journey so long

Will be filled with solid training
PT, knowledge and drill
As they strengthen their bodies
And sharpen their skill

But the chaos that follows
Is what I most dread
Will they withstand
The games played in their heads?

I can't help but wonder
I can only surmise
That our recruits will respond
To our great surprise

Learning their bearings

Trying not to unfold
As they endure the hardships
Many of which untold

Just when they think
That they did something right
The DI responds
Giving recruits another fright

But what can I do
As I sit here and ponder?
Nothing, I'm told
But I still have to wonder

I take to my knees
And focus — and pray
Give strength to my recruit
And show them the way

The next day will come
And I won't hear a word
As my friends try to tell me
I must rest assured

Bribing the mailman
Won't make word come quicker
And the federal government
Frowns on me offering him liquor

One day he'll bring me
A letter so short
But I'll cherish it dearly
As I write a retort

I know what I'll do
I'll pick up a pen
I'll write another letter
Again and again

He needs them more
Than I need from him
I might even include
His favorite hymn

Maybe a picture
Or a news clipping from home
To let my recruit know
That he is not alone

The day to remember

This was the morning
We met our DIs
One of the only times
I looked in their eyes

As the CO introduced them
I saw stern leaders
Tall, strong, and bulky
Giant as cedars

The DI oath been recited
That moment of quiet
Before the Senior gave a speech
And then — quite a riot

The DIs went crazy
Flailing about
With every command
All we could do was shout

Aye aye sir
At the top of our lungs
Voices going hoarse
Throats have now stung

Immediate obedience
Is all that they ask
But the confusion that follows
Every single task

Learning a new language
Like "get on line" and "cover down"
Do it wrong
And they do more than just frown

Will this day ever end

I see it on everyone's faces
But someone just messed up
Tying his boot laces

The chaos restarts
With a renewed sense of rigor
These DIs certainly have
Plenty of vim and vigor

Finally chow time
Maybe get a break
Eat really quickly
And now a stomach ache

A moment of free time
Just an hour each night
Gather your thoughts
Think about your plight

Write home to Mom
She must be worried sick
Shortest of letters
No time — be quick

Just let her know you're ok
And the food here is common
Nutritious and healthy
But better than ramen

"I love you, Mom"
Written large and bold
Hoping this gives her
Comfort untold

Sign off tonight
Training day one is tomorrow
I've got this, Mom
Put aside your sorrow

Are you all right?

My dearest recruit
Are you all right?
I hear you're at medical
Don't give me a fright

You left me in perfect health
Why all of the fuss?
Can't the doctors pass you by
Is this really a must?

You're big, strong, and healthy
Tall, handsome, and lean
Are the doctors and nurses
Really that mean?

To put you through another
Medical examination
That repetition after MEPS
Seems an odd combination

You'd think they'd just look
At the papers they'd given you
Say 'this one's good'
And move you down the queue

But sometimes logic escapes me
When I hear what's at stake
They're keeping you moving
Every moment you're awake

With medical and dental
Taken in stride
But what was that shot
They put in your backside?

Ouch that had to hurt

I hope you can take it
And if it's really too painful
You'll probably need to fake it

Don't let them see your pain
It'll make you look shoddy
Besides, pain they told you
Is weakness leaving the body

Now off you go
To pick up more gear
Be careful how you march
With that pain in your rear

I miss Doc Jones

Dear Mom, what a day
We had over at medical
They poked and they prodded
Then sent me to dental

They put us in lines
A million yards long
To test us and check us
To see if we're strong

Ready for the rigors
Of training ahead
What they're going to do today
Is what I most dread

First up for all of us
Is immunization
The nurses are kind
But their prime obligation

Is to move us through
The herd-like setting
It's nowhere near done
I'm certainly betting

Next is a blood test
A few vials have been drawn
The one who had fainted
Was the one with most brawn

Say 'ah,' turn your head
Lift one leg, now bend over
The only thing we haven't done
Is play a game of Red Rover

And now over to dental

But they pull us aside
And put a 'peanut butter'
Into our backside

Holy $#@+ that was painful
But I better stand up right
If the DI sees me in pain
It'll be a long night

Finally to dental
Where they poke and they prod
Nearly finished, I'm told
Almost done, thank God

The last thing's an X-ray
To check on my bones
I must say, Mom
I miss Doctor Jones

Can you hear me?

Recruit, can you hear me
Calling your name
Your hearing test underway
My heart is aflame

Knowing you're concentrating
In that soundproof room
Just press it when you hear it
Don't try to assume

The beeps will be heard
Ignore your heartbeat
Try to keep still
Don't even tap your feet

Hearing test all finished
You're doing quite fine
I'm proud of you already
Keep holding the line

Beeps through the thumps

The strangest thing yet
That they've made us endure
Is a hearing test
In a booth, quiet and demure

The headsets we wore
Were as tight as a vice
And then some had to
Go through it at least twice

But the thumping rhythm
Of our beating hearts
Pulsating our heads
Before the test would start

Made us wonder what we'll hear
When it got underway
Oh...tiny beeping
The easiest part of the day

So I passed this test
There was nothing to dread
But I can't help wondering
What next lies ahead

Don't worry for tomorrow
The Bible reminds me
Concentrate for now
Where the need really finds me

IST: The Next Acronym

IST
Initial Strength Test
To prove you're ready
To train with the best

At least three times
Get up over that bar
Pull-ups galore
Will get you quite far

Down on your back
Give me 80 crunches
When we finish here
To the chow hall for lunches

But first you must pass
The last bit of 'fun'
Now it is time
For a mile and a half run

Get through these three
Hold your head high and steady
Prove to the DIs
That this recruit is now ready

Time to show them

Dear Mom, now it's time
To work through the pain
The Initial Strength Test
Proves I'm ready to train

Dressed in PT gear
By dawn's early light
Endurance and speed
Determination and might

Are needed this morning
If I'm to move on
And meet my DIs
At the barracks over yon

But first I need
To get three pull-ups on high
Chin over the bar
And then to stand by

Next to the ground
With my feet held by a buddy
The cool morning dew
Makes my back a bid muddy

No time for distraction
Gotta get crunches at least 80
While my buddy holds my legs down
To make it quite weighty

And now for the final test
A mile and a half jog
Down traffic-free streets
Through misty morning fog

I gave it my all

Quite certain I passed
No, I wasn't first
But definitely not last

Slugging down the water
From my newly issued canteen
You can tell which recruits
Are addicted to caffeine

It seems we all passed
Our recruiters were right
Train well in advance
And you'll be ready to fight

This first test of our abilities
We now leave behind
There's a long way to go
Before we are completely refined

Now for the rifle

Today you pick up
One last piece of gear
Your M-16 rifle
But you've nothing to fear

This is your new best friend
The legendary poems entail
Keep it clean and ready
And it will never fail

Your father taught you
How to handle firearms right
But some of your buddies
Might have a look of fright

Do what you can
To help them pay attention
To learn what they need
To ease all their tension

It's only a tool
Placed in the proper hands
Used to protect
Our sacred homelands

For now listen carefully
To all that you need
Learn about your rifle
And memorize the rifleman's creed

My beautiful rifle

I got my M-16 rifle
Clean, sleek, and black
Used for defense
And also for attack

But also for drill
As we learn to get sharp
Hold that piece right!
The DIs now harp

New movements we learn
Like right shoulder arms
Master the cadence
No cause for alarm

Take it apart
Put it back together
Clean it thoroughly
Protect it from bad weather

Keep it beautiful
Give her a name
Something unique
That no one else can claim

I figured it out
This rifle is like no other
So I'll give her the same name
As my dear precious mother

First Sunday

My first Sunday on the island
Only a week — it seems longer
But now to the chapel
To make my soul stronger

The DI that marched us
Has a different look on his face
His kindness toward us
As we enter this place

Has me wondering what happened
To the Marine, tough and lean
Standing before God
He's not at all mean

The Chaplain encourages
Every single recruit
To keep their faith together
And let it bear fruit

The message of today
Was on faith, hope, and love
It certainly resembled
A word from Above

How Great Thou Art
As we lift our lives to Him
And close out the service
With the Marine Corps hymn

Now back to the barracks
The DI would chime
Square things away
And take an hour of free time

Later this evening

The Senior sits down
Takes off his Smokey
And puts away his frown

It's time for instruction
Of a different kind
Informal information
To feed the hungry mind

Finally to chow
A shower and bed
Today made me realize
I don't have to dread

It's going to get rough
But I've done OK so far
Good night Chesty Puller
Wherever you are

Our first Sunday apart

A bittersweet Sunday
Is now in the book
And sitting in church
My spirit was shook

But the preacher assured us
It is well with our souls
In God's tender arms
Our loved ones He holds

When I went up front
For comfort and prayer
The whole church surrounded
To offer their care

They laid their hands upon me
And lifted their voices
Lord protect her recruit
Help him make the right choices

Someone broke out in song
Without prompting from any
And what I received
Was comfort aplenty

They took me to lunch
Even though I felt rather drab
And when it was over
They picked up the tab

This ones for the Corps
And for your Marine in the making
Encouragement like that
Kept my tired heart from breaking

Thank you, Heavenly Father

And protect him with Your might
I feel at peace now
Let me sleep through the night

Day 1 tomorrow

Looking at the schedule
Day One starts tomorrow
I've got to work through
The pain and the sorrow

My child is in Boot Camp
No longer a baby
Can I hold it together?
Yes, no...or maybe

Back to the support group
I need a word of hope
So many questions
I feel like a dope

Lynn and her team
Make the day go by easy
Even "Mayor" Clark Linden
With his jokes rather cheesy

What's that on my front porch
While my leaves I am raking
Someone sent me a yard flag
Marine in the Making

Praise God and thank you
For my brand new yard sign
Yellow footprints now adorn
The sidewalk's straight line

I needed that gift
It meant quite a lot
Just a small token of love
But what joy it has wrought

Strength for today

Bright hope for tomorrow
I now look forward
Training Day One is tomorrow

The starting line

Today is the day
They give us more stuff
Guidebooks and knowledge
Laid out on blankets so rough

Final gear check today
And tomorrow we start
Training Day One will prove
What lies in our hearts

It's mind over matter
They tell us each day
Tomorrow they test
If we mean what they say

Foot locker all packed
Everything that I own
Plus my rifle and boots
Lined up like we were shown

OPEN YOUR KNOWLEDGE
Comes the shout with a start
Breaking the silence
And jumping the heart

Just start reading the first chapter
Learn what you can
Use the time wisely
Read carefully — don't scan

Tomorrow we step out
Recruits — a new role
We even get to put
The yellow flag on our pole

Drill, Baby, Drill

Left, right
Left, right
Stay in rhythm
Keep it tight

The Junior DI
Calls one step at a time
Sometimes his cadence
Belts out a rhyme

Focusing each step
When someone goes wrong
Then a trip to the sand pit
Makes the lesson prolong

Try it again
Do it over and over
And back to the pits
To 'plant roses and clover'

Finally done right
The DI starts to shout
Not bad but nothing
To write home about

Try it again
Let's see if you got it
But someone messed up
And the DIs could spot it

Everyone give me pushups
Because you just blew it
You'll learn as a team
You will ALL work through it

Together as one

We learn close order drill
Plenty more to go
As we work on this skill

Dear Dad, I'm sorry

Dear Dad, I'm sorry
What I'm about to write
May cause you some angst
And anger you it might

But I cut off my hair
It was getting in the way
I hope you're not mad
Really hope, even pray

But the Corps demands
That our hair buns keep tight
And the first couple days
It was a horrible sight

I know you're not happy
As I write you explaining
It's only to save time
And focus on my training

I love you forever
Let there never be doubt
When I get to the fleet
I'll start to grow it out

Yes I'm working
To be a Marine in this world
But deep down inside
I'll always be your Baby Girl

Sweetheart, it's ok

My dear baby girl
Today I got your letter
And I hope my response
Will help you feel better

Regarding your hair
I knew it was coming
After getting your letter
I spent the day bumming

It's part of your beauty
Quite like no other
Curly and wavy
You look like your mother

But these days call for changes
And your appearance must alter
I'm more concerned with your training
Be sure you don't falter

So cut your hair short
Gel it down, comb it back
Your training matters more
And Dad has your back

Boot camp will separate
Contenders from players
Get up each day
To disprove the naysayers

Besides, short hair on you
Shouldn't look all that bad
You're beautiful as always
Signing off now, love, Dad

I've written three letters

I've written three letters
Since my child has been gone
The days go by quickly
But the nights are ever long

Picking up the paper
And a brand new blue pen
I'll write my recruit
Again and again

What now should I say
She's caught up on the news
I don't want to tell her
That I'm fighting the blues

Gotta get creative
Send a pic of the cat
Sprawled out completely
Asleep on the mat

An encouraging card
With an inspiring rhyme
A poem to read
During her hour of free time

Whatever the case
No excuse to be lazy
I've got to do something
To avoid going crazy

I love you, Recruit
You're unique, like no other
Be strong and courageous
Good night, dear. Love, Mother

The first letter home

My first letter home
Dear Mom and Dear Dad
Sometimes it's really rough
Other times it's not bad

For close order drill
The DIs we must copy
More often than not
We look really sloppy

Got to get it right
And stop making mistakes
Clearly causing
A number of headaches

Something just clicked
We finally got it right
One simple move
But not done for the night

Build on that victory
Create a foundation
So that on family day
There can be jubilation

But a long way to go
That much is certain
Going to march a lot more
Hope my feet don't start hurting

"Let's try a new move"
The DI raises his voice
We all shout "Aye, aye, sir!"
As if we had a choice

Now something I noticed

As our feet start to burn
His way of teaching...
He wants us to learn

It's not just a shouting match
Nor is it pure fright
The Corps is molding us
To learn to do right

So mind over matter
Is starting to kick in
Just keep your head on straight
And wipe off that stupid grin

Hope this letter amuses you
After your daily commute
Signing off for now
Love you always, your recruit

Tired and wired

I've not slept well
These past several nights
The postal employees
I keep in my sights

I come home from work
Completely uninspired
Not wanting to eat
One hundred percent tired

Hoping for a letter
Or a note from my recruit
But only junk mail
That my garbage can will pollute

Then in sit in the bed
Maybe watch a little TV
What is this rustling
Of papers I see?

Another bill I forgot
To file and to route
Or another bit of junk mail
I forgot to toss out?

Wait! It's an envelope
Not fancy but plain
Hand written in blue pen
I recognize the name

A LETTER at last!
I can now take it easy
But what if the contents
Make my spirit queasy?

Just open the letter

Don't worry what's written
The first thing he notes
How the sand fleas have bitten

Super short was his note
Telling me he's all right
Now will I be able
To sleep through the night?

Today was a day
That I was feeling quite dreary
But now with my letter
I'm now rather weary

Ready to sleep now
I know what I'll do
I'll make a new pouch
To help me get through

I'll store all my letters
In this pouch by my bed
So if I wake in the night
I can fill up my head

With the notes and the writings
That say, 'Mom don't you fear
I'll be ok
On this island over here.'

When I first got home
I was ever so tired
Now with this letter
I'm wide awake, even wired

But the body is worn out
Time for sleep, that is certain
Turn down the covers
Lower the curtain

Amazing to me
How a half page letter
Can put body and mind
In a state so much better

Gone is the worry
The dread and the fright
Pleasant dreams await me
As I sleep through the night

Dear Baby Sister

Dear Baby Sister
I'm writing to you only
During my free time
I sometimes feel lonely

I cannot imagine
You going without
Your big brother beside you
Please try not to pout

My days are quite busy
No time for thinking
But I miss the cherry colas
We used to be drinking

The times we spent
At the movies or the game
Now that we are apart
I'm sure they're not the same

The first day after boot camp
I'll spend with you, I promise
You have my word
Don't be a doubting Thomas

First thing in the morning
Until we've worn ourselves lazy
You plan the whole day
Go ahead, let's get crazy

A movie, the beach
Dinner and lunch
Bring a friend if you want
Bring a whole bunch

Or just you and me

We will spend the whole day
Burgers and cherry colas
The old fashioned way

I've just one request
It only seems fair
Would you send in a letter
A lock of your hair?

I'll keep it stored in my locker
Tucked away out of sight
But just to remind me
That you're doing all right

In the meantime, enclosed
Is something to wear around your hand
A bracelet for you
From me, a boot band

Decorate one how you like
But what of the other?
Please give the second one
To our dearest mother

I'm crying, big brother

I'm crying, big brother
Since I got your boot band
You thought of me
While suffering in the sand

I haven't stopped bawling
Since yesterday evening
The drops on the paper
Should keep you believing

The letter came in
As I sat down to dinner
Even in loneliness
To me, you're a winner

Your undying love
To me, your little sister
Has turned my poor heart
Into quite a strong twister

Love, joy, and sorrow
Are the start of my emotions
But pride tops them all
It's as deep as the oceans

If a lock of my hair
Would make you more happy
It makes perfect sense
It's not one bit sappy

I'm enclosing a picture
To go with the hair
But on our day out together
My big brother I won't share

I'll plan all the outings

Just you and just me
Thinking ahead
Fills my heart with some glee

Mom and I will work through this
We will somehow find a way
Looking forward to hugging you
On Family Day

Signing off for the night
You take care, big Mister
I love you forever
Your loving Baby Sister

That's my sweetheart

'Who's that in the picture?'
Asked another recruit
That's my dear sweetheart
Looking ever so cute

She sent me this picture
Printed from a selfie
Beautiful smile
Hair soft and silky

But what I love about her most
Is her sweet and kind soul
Her inner qualities
Are what I extol

She loves to help others
She gives without asking
Everyone she encounters
Should never be lacking

She puts up with my antics
And laughs at my jokes
She's even confided
That she loves my folks

Since the day I met her
My heart she has carried
After my first deployment
We're going to get married

For months she's been dreaming
Of being a Marine wife
She is committed to this
Crazed military life

So forgive me if I brag

From east through the west
But my beautiful sweetheart
Is simply the best

Hey, little brother

Hey, little bother
Mom tells me you're upset
Yes I'm far away
But you've nothing to fret

Finally you get
The bedroom to yourself
But do me a favor
Keep my stuff on the shelf

I'll be back in a few months
Keep the room nice and neat
Be good to our mother
And I'll take you out to eat

Or maybe a ballgame
A movie or two
You can decide
What we're going to do

But you have to be strong
For our mom and our sister
You're the man of the house now
You're the big mister

You need transportation
I know what you'd like
If you take good care of it
You can have my racing bike

Keep it secure
And tidy and clean
It'll serve you well
It's a fine machine

I gotta go now

Starting to get late
I'll be home soon enough
It'll be worth the wait

Give my love to our sister
And our dear precious mother
Keep some for yourself
I love you, your brother

Your first birthday away

I cannot believe
I'm writing today
On this, your first birthday
In a land far away

I'm proud of what you're doing
But my heart cannot take
Do I make your favorite dinner?
Do I bake you a cake?

The mind wanders back
To the day you were born
So much potential
In your tiny baby form

Now all grown up
Serving our great nation
Just knowing this
Is cause for celebration

So I'll invite your friends over
Your grandparents too
I'll make your special meal
And bake a cake just for you

Even though you can't join us
We'll celebrate on your behalf
And record it for later
As we pray, cry, and laugh

When you get home,
We will do it agin
And play back the videos
With all of your friends

Happy Birthday, recruit

We love you so dear
And look forward to having
You home oh so near

The amazing Dan Daly

Today in our classes
We learned a great lesson
An extraordinary Marine
With him there was no messin

His name was Dan Daly
At the time he was a Gunny
What he did at Bellau Wood
Was certainly not funny

But even before that
He received two medals of honor
The tales of his heroics
Are far from a yawner

The Boxer Rebellion
Where he got his first award
Holding off 200 enemies
While the victory he scored

In 1915
In the battle of Haiti
He and 40 Marines
Held off over three eighty

And then out in France
His rally cry was quite clever
"Come on, you sons of bitches,
Do you want to live forever?"

Yes, it's strong language
But they're training us to be mean
We're every one preparing
To be a badass Marine

He was offered a commission

But turned it down twice
His hearty response
Was not very nice

He told Smedley Butler
When he rejected the offer
I'd rather be an outstanding sergeant
Than just another officer

These are the Marines
Who lead by example
And the first couple classes
Are only a sample

One thing is certain
As we hear of each feat
The US Marine Corps
Is the world's most elite

I'm telling you this, Mom
You have permission, you're allowed
When I've earned the title Marine
You have a right to be proud

Training to fight

Day Four in my training
And what is up next
Martial arts for today
But I'm feeling quite vexed

I've never fought anyone
Like they're about to demonstrate
Got to pay full attention
And not hesitate

One mind any weapon
Adorns the top of the barn
Where we listen and learn
On how to disarm

Take the instructors
Lessons fully to heart
Prepare for the testing
That will play a huge part

One of the many tests
I will take while I am here
But to pass this test
I must use brain, eyes, and ears

It's not just strength
And physical might
Spirit and wisdom
Also help win the fight

Don't worry, Mom
We won't be easily rattled
But victory is ours
When we're called into battle

This training is more

Than learning to survive
Clearly the Corps
Expects us to thrive

I did pretty well
Except for the one bruise and welt
I'll make you so proud
When I earn my tan belt

Breakfast on the island

Breakfast on the island
Or as we call morning chow
Is the best time of day
And I think I know how

Weekdays was normally
Cereal and toast
But then every Sunday,
Of Dad's breakfasts we'd boast

Bacon and eggs
Biscuits and gravy
Hearty meals like Grandpa
Had in the Navy

It'd fill us up
Make us ready for the day
No complaints about hunger
As our tasks we now slay

Not quite as delicious
As you or Dad would make
But it feels nice to eat
Something good once we wake

So don't worry, Mom
I'm not getting scrawny
Between food and PT
I'm getting rather brawny

Just one request
My first morning home, if you please
Have Dad make an omelette
With bacon — and lots of cheese

Holidays on the island

Whatever the holiday
I really don't care
I'm here at home
And you're over there

Fourth of July
Christmas or Thanksgiving
What are you doing
How are you living?

Is there any celebration
Fancy chow for dinner
If so, gobble up
Don't want you getting thinner

Will there be fireworks
Or a short time of prayer
Tell me, I need to know
What you're doing over there

We are celebrating at home
But it's just not the same
Without our recruit
But our candle is aflame

We are praying and planning
For when you get back
We will celebrate in style
Food and fun we won't lack

But it's hard to celebrate
While we are apart
Find comfort in this letter
Written straight from the heart

First hike

I'm worn out and sore
From our very first hike
Only 5K was the distance
We all made it, even Mike

Mike is my rack mate
Really cool guy
From North Carolina
He's a little bit shy

But we really hit if off
And we needed each other
To make it through the day
He's just like a brother

How do we get through
These marches so grueling
Encourage each other
And protein bars for fueling

We are learning to help
Each other without asking
While we march and encourage
Our way of multitasking

We had to keep moving
No room for any stopping
We saw to it that no one
Was in danger of dropping

With brethren like these
We will all be OK
We have each other's backs
Come whatever that may

As the sun goes down...

Marching back from chow
We can see the sun set
Broken only by
A single sleek fighter jet

From the nearby air base
Where Marines are in the fleet
Serving our country
Greasy arms, tired feet

But something struck me
As we march a straight line
Mom, you see the same sunset
And tonight it's mighty fine

Though miles separate us
And a few state borders
The beauty of a setting sun
Sets my heart and mind in order

I know you're still with me
Praying to God above
The last warm rays of the sun
Have transferred your love

I'm calm and relaxed now
The day nearly done
Shower, shave, and write a letter
To my favorite one

Attention to detail
Paid off tonight
Good night, dearest mother
Relax now — sleep tight

Sharing our sunset

Yes, my recruit
I saw the sun set
And that night it was one
Of the most beautiful yet

I stood on our porch
Looking west and thinking
What's happening to him now
While the sun is low-sinking

I don't know what to do
So I kneel down and pray
God send him my love
With a warm, soft sun ray

How it came over me
To do what you had felt
I will never understand
But that God's love has been dealt

A letter like that
Lets me know you're succeeding
I can rest better at night
When my heart isn't speeding

Tough days are ahead
Of that I am sure
For you and for me
And there really is no cure

But we forge ever forward
To challenges unknown
Until Liberty Sunday
When you call me on the phone

And then I'll know for sure

You've made through and I can shout
He's now a Marine
I never had any doubt

Until that day
That you finally earn your place
Take every ray of sun
As a kiss on your face

My Waldo!

I found him! I FOUND HIM!
I finally found my Waldo
He looks so handsome
But completely bald, oh no!

There's no mistaking
Among recruits with their pimples
I can see it's my son
No mistaking those dimples

He's taller than most
But he's put on some muscle
You can see in his face
He has heart, he has hustle

What are they doing
With their rifles and gear?
How did the photographer
Get ever so near?

That we could see in detail
Our sons and our daughters
Crossing roadways and bridges
Trenches and waters

Now I will print
This picture so grand
And frame it and hang it
What a handsome young man

Hoping these pictures
Will bring comfort to others
Thank you for posting
From us recruit mothers

A pile of letters

Sweetheart, I know
That boot camp is lonely
And I'm certain it's worse
For those recruits who only

Get one letter a week
Or none whatsoever
So you're about to get slammed
With a huge pile of letters

I talked to our pastor
And he to the congregation
About how neat it would be
To represent a grateful nation

So each member of the church
Took a few minutes time
And wrote down some notes
Drew a picture or some rhyme

Getting all their names
Would only encumber
So each is addressed
To 'Recruit Laundry Number'

That way everyone
In Platoon forty-thirteen
Hears an encouraging phrase
Each treated like a queen

Perhaps a new friendship
Can take hold and stand fast
You never know of the bond
And how long they will last

But for now, your platoon mates

Can enjoy this short rhyme
And a pile of letters
During tonight's free time

So what's on TV

So what's on TV?
Is there anything good?
Give me an update
About our neighborhood

Did they fix that pothole?
Did the Jones's move away.
Or have they decided
To finally stay?

What of Timmy next door
Has he learned how to walk
Or has cerebral palsy
Continued to stalk?

You remember Sarah
She asked me to assist
In getting in shape
Did she finally enlist?

Has Mr. Watson given
His two weeks notice
To retire from teaching
And drive away in a Lotus?

What other news
Can you tell me in a letter?
Give it to me straight
Don't try to make it better

I need to hear bad news
As well as the good
Let me hear all the facts
Give it straight like you should

The reason I wanted

To get all the news
I want to hear good things
I need to hear the blues

And what about sports
Have my Birds given in?
While the Yankees and Red Sox
Know only how to win?

For just a few minutes each night
I want my mind to roam
About the comings and goings
Happening back home

Then tomorrow I will focus
On the many tasks at my hand
Are you still wearing
My little green boot band?

Thanks for everything
Your love and support
Gives me strength and encouragement
It never stops short

Something to do...

What do I do
To prevent an idle mind
While my recruit is away
In boot camp's heavy grind?

I can't sit around
Feeling sorry for myself
After cleaning the house
And putting her picture on the shelf

Got to avoid
The dread and the bore
Maybe I'll join
Team Healthy Corps

It's full of Marines,
Parents and veterans
There's no other group
That I'll fit better in

So I'll sign up right now
Clean my sneakers and sweats
Surely getting fit
Won't come with regrets

My recruit is working
Every day in PT
They say it's good for you
So it must be good for me

More than just workouts
We work on body and mind
And important growth
Of the spiritual kind

No judgment from anyone

That much is clear
Just encouraging words
From everyone here

In the next couple months
When she returns from the range
She'll notice immediately
That something has changed

We transformed together
Though miles apart
United in purpose
In mind and in heart

Some news for you

Here are some news clippings
I thought you would like
Focusing on the good news
So your emotions don't spike

As you can see
One of your friends got married
What really was funny
Was how the bride he had carried

The football team
Is doing much better
And the quarterback just signed
A big commitment letter

He's going to Nebraska
To learn how to play
In hopes he can make it
To the NFL one day

Your baby sister got awarded
At the 4-H last week
For her creative recipes
Both tasty and unique

I've even included
The comic strip funnies
Don't laugh too loudly
Or you'll draw out the Gunnys

Pass these around
To your fellow recruits
During your free time
While cleaning your boots

I hope you enjoyed

And found it clever
Signing off for now
I love you forever

I'm done with work

I'm done with work
I've plopped in my chair
Time to put up the feet
And let down my hair

The office has got me
Going every which way
New product releases
Going out on display

Tons of angry clients
Too many to call
Help whom I can
But can't get to them all

A moment of pity
And a little self doubt
Led me to realize
What this life is about

While my recruit is up training
In a Carolina swamp
I'm out here complaining
Looking down with great pomp

Life could be worse
As I sit near the couch
While my recruit has her dinner
MREs in a pouch

While I read about celebrities
And their antics all droll
She's out in the field
Learning combat patrol

I realize then

I don't need that manure
While Marines in the Making
Learn to keep us secure

So while my recruit
Is working on her training
I'll learn what I can
To stop my complaining

Italian Battalion

Greetings, dear Mom
From the Fourth Battalion
Something strange today
We all ate Italian

Don't get any ideas
It's not what you're thinking
I haven't gone AWOL
And I haven't been drinking

But tonight in the field
As we all grabbed our rations
Our meals were the same
Each after one fashion

Meatballs in red sauce
With garlic potatoes and mash
We were all quite hungry
Nothing went to the trash

But MREs should be different
No two are alike
Full variety in the cases
To swap what we don't like

It even had breadsticks
And jalapeño cheddar cheese
Just open the pouch
And give it a squeeze

Strange mixing Mexican
And Italian cuisines
But that's how they do it
As United States Marines

Beef sticks for the next hike

When we rest our tired feet
And a pouch with some cookies
When we want something sweet

Nowhere near as tasty
When you rattle the pan
But better than expected
Or eating out of a can

Run with me

Up in the morning
With the rising sun
Come on, Mom
Let's go for a run

I'm in boot camp
And you're at home
But that doesn't mean
We can't let our minds roam

We PT every morning
Just as the sun pokes out
So at the same time
You can get up and about

And while I am running
With platoon thirty sixty-two
I'll imagine I'm running
Alongside of you

You don't really have
To go very long
Just a little each day
To help you get strong

Even a half mile walk
Sets the tone for the day
Clear the mind, tone the body
And be on your way

I'm not asking this of you
To make you feel bad
This suggestion is here
To make you more glad

Then our PT sessions

Won't seem like a grind
While we are apart
We are still of one mind

My time away
May seem like forever
But when I get home
We can go running together

All about honor

Today in core values
We learned of a trait
That puts everyone in charge
Of his own daily fate

Of the big three they teach us
Honor, Courage, and Commitment
Our Senior DI
Let us know what it all meant

This lesson number one
On a bright Sunday evening
Honor was most vital
We are all now believing

The word honor is in our hymn
That we have to keep it clean
If we are to obtain
The title of Marine

It goes hand in hand
With integrity and truth
To give us wisdom beyond years
And the innocence of youth

We learned today
Honors more than not crooking
It's doing the right thing
Even when no one is looking

Even the Air Force
Believes 'integrity first'
Now we all realize
After honor we must thirst

It was an easy lesson to learn

With my boot camp comrades
Because of what I've been taught
By you and by Dad

Rest assured though that this class
Was by no means a yawner
Good to get a refresher
When it's all about honor

Pugil sticks

Today was the day
We had pugil stick fights
Adrenaline rush by day
And later bruises tonight

But don't worry, Mom
It was really quite fun
They taught us to fight
We have no reason to run

The first blow landed
Upside of my head
But I stayed in the ring
And came out swinging instead

No one got hurt
No one's tails were draggin'
It was safely conducted
No need for the meat wagon

They'd put out a huge recruit
Against one with skin and bone
To make sure that everyone
Could hold up their own

The smaller ones did well
Though severely outmatched
Even one smaller recruit
Made the other's helmet detach

Yes, it was grueling
But also rather fun
Even this early in boot camp
We're fighting as one

So I can see how this training

Unites us together
When we graduate boot camp
We'll be brothers forever

Please don't get hurt

The struggle I'm having
With this letter I write
Is whether you get hurt
When you're training to fight

When you were a toddler
I kept the house safe
The biggest danger back then
Was occasional diaper chafe

And while you were school aged
Life wasn't a breeze
You'd fall off your bike
Or skin both your knees

Then on into high school
You played plenty of sports
I sat in the stands worried
From injuries of all sorts

Those I could handle
I had some control
But now you're in boot camp
And your hand I can't hold

Those high obstacles
Give me cause for alarm
If you should fall off
You would surely break your arm

Yes I get worried
I'm your mother, after all
It would tear my heart in pieces
If you should take a fall

So please don't get hurt

And I don't even mean maybe
Though you a grown adult
You'll always be my baby

Into the sand

'Get down on your faces'
Our DI did bellow
As we entered the sand pit
He rolled up the yellow

Our guidon was tied up
With several boot bands
The platoon was in trouble
Everyone in the sand

We messed up today
During close order drill
We just didn't have it
And now the DIs are all shrill

Jumping jacks, push-ups
Burpees by the dozens
This is more grueling
Than farming with our cousins

Then they shout STOP
And we start to catch our breath
But someone heaved a sigh
And now we have the look of death

They didn't care who but shouted
'BACK ON YOUR FACES
Mountain climbers! Push the dirt!
You're off to the races!'

It's gotta end soon
Or so it would seem
One recruit messes up
And they punish the whole team

Finally we are out

'This time do it right'
As they march us again
And we give all our might

Finally we halted
And the DI did shout
'That wasn't too bad
 Nothing to write home about'

We let out an Ooh-RAH!
Our instinct kicked in
I half wonder if I saw
The DI crack a grin

What changed in that eternity
That we spent in the sands?
Something clicked within us
As they shouted commands

We started to listen
And react as a team
The better we did
They less they would scream

It's not Pavlov's dog
That we are being treated
It's learning in everything
How to not be defeated

We will get through this
If each pulls his weight
Just wait and see
We're going to be great!

Need a favor

Hey, big sister
I need a huge favor
If you could help
You'd be a life saver

I'd love a new pen pal
A friend from your platoon
Someone with whom
I can help stay in tune

Not really a girlfriend
But someone to share
Encouraging words
One for whom I can care

If you know a recruit
Who has no one to write
Give her my address
I'll make it all right

Not wanting to be creepy
Or even score a date
Just think it'd be nice
To help your rack mate

To avoid being lonely
By getting no mail
And keeping her heart
From getting too frail

That way I can know
How to pray for you both
So you can get stronger
Wherever you need growth

I want to give friendship

To you and another
So do a big favor
To your best little brother

My new friend

I have a new friend
Though we've known him for years
Our local postal employee
Helps get rid of my fears

He brings me your letters
Every once in a while
And when he does
It sure makes me smile

When I'm not stalking
His horn he will honk
But if there are no letters
I threaten to bonk

It's all in good fun
I know it's not his fault
But I'd love to hear daily
To prevent an assault

So the more often you write
Your mother back home
The safer the mail man
Will remain on the roam

Do you need envelopes
Stamps or a pen
No excuses just write me
Again and again

A half page letter
Is all that I need
And one even longer
Would be a good deed

So write every day

As often as you can
That's the safest way
To preserve the mail man

Up over the head

Today we did log lifts
It didn't look easy
But lifting together
It became rather breezy

Paying full attention
And using extra care
We hoisted the pole
High into the air

Up from the ground
Now onto our shoulders
It's starting to feel
Like we are lifting large boulders

Over our heads
To the other side
Hands getting sweaty
It's starting to slide

'Get a grip on it you'
The DI screamed out
Someone let go
Come on, man, don't pout

This thing's really heavy
Don't hesitate
It always gets lighter
If we all lift the weight

A hard lesson was learned
But not through screaming DIs
Everyone must contribute
No matter his size

They told us on day one

We would train as a team
This morning was no exception
They were right it would seem

MCX Call

After our haircuts
Shaven again, bald
Off to Recruit MCX
To buy quite a haul

Three cans of shave gel
Six packs of razors
You'd think we were shaving
Our faces with lasers

Toothpaste and toothbrush
Enough for three weeks
Keep the teeth shiny
Healthy tongue and clean cheeks

New pair of running shoes
We've worn the first pair out
From PT and fire watch
And running about

Clean t-shirts and silkies
What you call gym shorts
Amazing how fast they fade
Doing sports of all sorts

Bleach, dryer sheets
And laundry detergent
For when uniforms get filthy
And cleaning is urgent

Stuff to wash windows
And scrub down the floors
And Brasso to polish
The brass on the doors

A scuzz brush to sweep down

The decks every morning
Bang three times then start sweeping
To give the dirt a warning

It's our job to keep tidy
Wherever we live
This isn't the Air Force
Maid service they don't give

What are these bands
With small silver hooks?
And this enormous green
Monster sized notebook?

And for our laundry bag
This 6-inch 'safety pin'
I thought of the Flintstones
And started to grin

The names here are strange
Learning a foreign tongue
Like ink sticks and go fasters
These new words they've flung

Aqua Velva, I don't get it
What could this be for
Someone just told me
It's for cleaning the floor

What insanity they've wrought
Here in boot camp
No wonder when drunk
They wear shades from a lamp

My ditty bag is full now
Paying with my EZ Pay Card
Almost forgot the moon beam
Feel like I left a junk yard

Confidence Course

At the Confidence Course
We made quite a racket
Some of the obstacles
Were on Full Metal Jacket

Stairway to Heaven
Scared me the most
A giant wooden ladder
Made of towering posts

Two by two you climbed it
Never looking down
Because if you did
Your head would spin round

Then to the A-frame
Three obstacles in one
Climb ropes and walk logs
Shimmy a tower for fun

Run jump and swing
Over a four foot trench
Then grab a canteen
Quickly make your thirst quench

The strangest of monkey bars
I now had to climb
The angle reversed
Get up quickly, no time!

The signature obstacle
Causes a fair share of strife
This beautiful artwork
Is called the Slide for Life

Climb a rope ladder

Formed like a large net
Go quickly and carefully
You're halfway up yet

Navigate more logs
Up over the ground
Then up another A-frame
And at the top you'll be found

Now to the ropes
Where you mount up head first
The water below beckons
'Fall in, and you're cursed'

A third of the way down
And flip yourself over
Pay attention to what you're doing
When you make the turnover

Two thirds down
Comes the trickiest part
Swing the feet out in front
Do it right, don't lose heart

Now that you've turned
Your whole body around
Shimmy the rest of the way
Down to solid ground

Those who fall in
Are fully soaking wet
And they have to come out
With their hands on their head

Paying full attention
And being a good listener
Means you come away dry
Not a dripping wet prisoner

On the way back
We did a short run
I have to admit, Mom
That was really fun

Gas, gas, GAS!

This morning was far
From what I wanted
No one could warn me
How much I felt haunted

As we filed by the dozens
To a dark chamber filled with gas
At first it wasn't bad
Until we took off the masks

The sting in our throats
And burning in in our eyes
Unmistakable was the feeling
How I wished for open skies

DON, CLEAR, AND CHECK
Came the next command
Was relief in sight?
Not from where I stand

The first test was easy
Learning again how to breathe
The harder part came after
When more gas began to seethe

'Get 'em off and start to sing
Our beloved Marine Corps Hymn'
And then a few jumping jacks
Wait, this isn't a gym

'Now get out of my chamber
The instructor did shout
As we moved one by one
Until the last of us was out

But oh what a sight

And the sounds of our hacks
Some lost all bearing
Felt like a chemical attack

Finally fresh air
And a bit of sunshine
Clean up your faces
And then get in line

What's next after this
No one can tell
I hope it's better
Than this hour of hell

One new advantage
After running like hoses
Since the day we arrived
We all have clear noses

The tower

The afternoon training
With our voices still hoarse
Brought something more frightening
Than the Confidence Course

A forty foot tower
Standing tall in the sun
Was intimidating from the ground
But it also looked fun

'Every recruit will go down
My tower at least twice!
Pay attention to me
Or you'll pay a heavy price!'

'Tie up the harness
Put the helmet on you gourd'
Safety was paramount
It struck quite a chord

Grab your gloves and start climbing
The tall tower's stairs
And jokingly a DI asked
'Do you have any heirs?'

Looking over I saw the Chaplain
Getting ready to mount
I thought if he could do it
I should make this one count

Down the free fall I jumped
Oh what a ride
Seemed like forever
Before the rope caught my side

Extend out the arm

Control your descent
And touch down on the ground
Now feeling content

Climb once again
The tower so tall
This time go down
The simulated wall

Second part of the day
Was better than the first
I'll take rappelling anytime
Gas chamber is the worst

Did I mention be safe?

With your last couple letters
I'm now worried sick
You're fighting each other
With large fighting sticks?

And what's with this chamber
Filled with noxious gas?
I swear if you get sick
I'll come kick your ... you know

If that's not enough
You jump off a tower
And when the day is done
Just a two minute shower?

After all you've been doing
I'd have thought you'd earned the right
To a long hot shower
Before you call it a night

But run everywhere
So you can stand in a line
Marine Corps logic escapes me
Much of the time

You wrote of a green monster
But you're not at Fenway Park
And how can you carry a moonbeam
When marching in the dark?

All this new jargon
Hits me like a freighter
When you get home
I might need a translator

Did I mention be safe

And look out below
I'm proud of you more
Than you'll ever know

The big "O"

Time to march over
And now off we go
To the obstacle course
Sometimes called the Big 'O'

From a distance it doesn't
Look intimidating
But getting up closer
We see what is waiting

Those logs are kind of high
The bars far apart
This takes speed and strength
But also courage and heart

First over a short log
And then a high bar
Got to jump just to catch it
Then swing my leg wide and far

A diagonal bar
Feet up like a jackknife
Then shimmy halfway down
Like the slide for life

The rest of the way
Down atop another log
Just getting above it
My speed it did bog

Next a set of boards
Resembling a wall
Didn't seem too tough
It was just six feet tall

More logs in the way

Close together I count six
But they're so close to each other
Getting through takes some tricks

A double bar awaits me
Over both I have to climb
Unlike the single
It's more difficult this time

Short logs between everything
I must jump
They're pretty thick, too
Wider than an oak stump

Finally at the end
A rope-climb to the top
When I touch the crossbar
Only then can I stop

Rank and name do I shout
At the top of my voice
Got to do it again
I don't have any choice

Our Senior DI
Staff Sergeant Crusher
Said that was too slow
Only worthy of the flusher

So do it again
With speed and with force
Finish it quickly
This obstacle course

The Grand Old Man

Today we have learned
In academic classes
About another Marine
Among the Badasses

The biggest surprise
To our listening ears
He served as Commandant
Thirty-nine years

Fifty-three years
He served in our Corps
Not a single Marine
Had ever served more

At one point he needed
To sound a loud klaxon
To oppose an idea
By President Jackson

Join with the Army
Was the proposal that day
Henderson and Congress
Told the White House 'no way!'

In 1843, he pinned
A note on his door
'Gone to Florida
Be back after the war'

Changing the Corps' mission
Is his greatest legacy
Our mission to fight
In air, on land, and sea

Archibald Henderson
Was a giant of a man
Forever now known
As the Corps' Grand Old Man

SDI Inspection

Holy Hades, what was that
We just now endured?
Inspection like no other
We are far from assured

Shaken to our boots
After later reflection
On the schedule it's called
Series Commander Inspection

Our first taste of pure failure
Now we know what it's like
It was louder than thunder
Quick as a lightning strike

The DIs were all over me
Pointing out all of my flaws
Shredding my confidence
Like a thousand buzz saws

When finished with me
And to the next recruit
They laid into him
About how he tied his boots

Nobody's perfect
Try as we might
But this time around
We got nothing right

The end of the whirlwind
Shook us to our core
Clearly we needed
To learn something more

The primary lesson
Through the screaming and blaring
Was grace under pressure
To keep your own bearing

That part we passed
One way or another
But deep down inside
I wanted my mother

One other lesson
In the midst of the rumble
After achieving so much
We have to be humble

Overconfidence can harm you
In life and in battle
Now I see the bigger purpose
But i still feel rattled

So today's exercise
Was mentally tough
The Corps making certain
We have the right stuff

Our second hike

A longer hike this time
Off to the races
From what I can tell
They picked up our paces

Despite the higher speed
It took us a while
This time the distance
Was not quite five miles

And more in our packs
They said we must haul
'Finish together
Everyone of you all'

The pace slightly quicker
And packs a bit heavy
I had an easier time
Pushing Grandpa Luke's Chevy

But press on we did
In the heat slightly searing
'Close it up, heel to toe!'
The DIs were sneering

Halfway through, a quick stop
Check our feet, drink some water
'Now let's go, move it out!'
As the sun just got hotter

Stay in tight help encourage
Each one and the others
We're in this together
Becoming like brothers

A new path we had taken
Didn't notice round the bend
But then saw our barracks
We just reached the end

'Change your socks and your boots
There's chow to be had!'
That got me to thinking

The hike wasn't that bad

Free time is over
Into our racks we all leap
One thing is certain
It'll be easy to sleep

Good night, Mom, I love you
And I love our sacred Corps
You most of all
Are worth fighting for

You still have this

I got your letter
About failing inspection
And it's time for your thoughts
To take up collection

In all of my years
One thing I have learned
Failure is far from
The path to get burned

Fall down seven times
You must get up eight
Trust me when I say
Of this there's no debate

Look for the lesson
From the problem at hand
Find where you can improve
And finally withstand

The slings and the arrows
You're facing right now
Last only a moment
For you to learn how

That when hardships befall you
And you want to give out
The one thing you don't do
Is sit around and pout

There's a balance between
Learning and navel gazing
After all, it's Marines
Your DIs are raising

So stand up, be strong
You'll pull this one through
And know that at all times
I'm praying for you

'Their courage, honor
Strength and skill
Their land to serve

Thy law fulfill'

Those words in the Navy Hymn
About Marines they do sing
Let it serve to remind you
When the chapel bell starts to ring

This Sunday when you worship
And kneel down to pray
Get your strength and your courage
To start another day

Big test, stay focused

I see on the schedule
Is a major test of skill
Last day of Phase One
Ending in Initial Drill

So my word to you today
Is stay focused and steady
You've trained every day
I'm sure you are ready

Listen carefully to the DI's
Every command
And when at attention
Tall you must stand

Keep your eyes fixed forward
And your cover on straight
Go into the steps
And don't hesitate

As the DI calls cadence
In his strong, steady beat
Stay in step every moment
As you put down your feet

Every movement, every step
Do them strong, do them loud
And though I can't be there so see it
Know in advance we are all proud

Looking forward to hearing
The results of your days
Next time I write you
You'll be in the Second Phase

Into the water!

This morning a large pool
Greeted our arrival
It's time to be amphibious
And learn water survival

Into the water
Please wish me luck
And pray for each one
Of the iron ducks

Recruits who can't swim
Or ever jumped in a pool
Some never learned
Now it seems rather cruel

But we have to all know
How to survive in the waters
If we're to be Sons of Chesty
Or one of his daughters

Those of us who can swim
To the diving platform
Proper jumping technique
We have to perform

Up to the top
Standing ready and bold
Step off, cross feet
HOLY COW! That water's cold!

Now swim to the area
They want us to tread
Ten minutes in the deep end
Isn't too much to dread

Next up is the test
Jumping in with full gear
Big, deep breath, jump right in
See? There's nothing to fear

For those who want Recon
Must learn more than survive
This training is the start
How in the water we thrive

John just came out
Of the Iron Duck side
He's got enough confidence
To give it a ride

Some of the recruits
Who have already passed
Are cheering him on
Hoping that he will last

While other recruits
In the pool's shallow end
See that John was successful
So now others ascend

Up the platform
Some sixty feet tall
If you jump as instructed
It won't seem like a fall

The trainers are there
To help you along
Just apply what they taught you
And don't be headstrong

At last, and at once
The last Iron Duck
Did it right using skill
No one needed any luck

Another requirement accomplished
Another skill set fully vital
Another day closer
To earning that title

Our money and our future

Today during swim week
We learned another skill
Not everything is PT
And close order drill

Now of our finances
We take full control
Learning how to prevent
Money falling in a hole

Retirement savings
Seems rather odd
Just a few weeks ago
Yellow footprints we've trod

But the future starts now
The financial sergeant teaches
Save now, go cheap
And keep your future in reaches

Sign up for Thrift Savings
To set money aside
For when our retirement
Would one day collide

Still, it's strange to be thinking
About compounded interest
And how a small bit of pay
Would be for our own best

And when they showed us the numbers
It started to make sense
A plan to retire comfortably
From the Department of Defense

If you want to avoid
Living life in a barrel
Save now for the future
Ignore at your peril

Sign me up, sir
Where is the dotted line
I understand now
That the future is mine

Kill it or die

The first attempt
At the CFT we tried
To pass it today
Or else we could die

The test is of speed
Of strength and of skill
Be quick and do it right
Our our enemy will kill

It starts out with a run
Around half a mile
I can already tell
This will be a heavy trial

Got to get through this
In three and a half minutes
To score really high
While the Corps tests my limits

Ammo can lifts
It's filled up with sand
Two minutes overhead
A thirty-pound can

Raise it 91 times
For a perfect score
Temps rising rapidly
As the sweat starts to pour

Maneuver under Fire
Like an obstacle course
But this time it's different
It takes more brute force

Sprint ten yards
Fifteen yard crawl
High and then low
Then a 'body' to haul

Grab two more cans
Sprint them through cones
Then toss a grenade
Make it land in the zone

Finally five pushups
Grab the cans one more time
Now sprint like a racehorse
To cross the finish line

Grab the water and report
'Recruit did his best!'
This ever important
Combat Fitness Test

Martial Arts Test

Today we will earn
Our first-level tan belts
But martial arts training
Can give us some welts

Never mind the pain
It's only temporary
And try to ignore
Your partner big and scary

If you follow the steps
You were earlier taught
You'll prove to the instructors
How hard you have fought

Every move, block, and jab
Be ready to recount
A little blood and some sweat
In no small amount

And now that we've passed
We can stand tall with pride
Don't forget to shake hands
Since we're on the same side

Courage

Another core values class
Our Senior DI gave us
This time about how
Courage can save us

Recounting the story
Of the Tripoli blockade
Overcoming the trap
The enemy had laid

And then of the exploits
In France's Belleau Wood
How Dan Daly and his troops
Had more than withstood

Iwo Jima, and Chesty
To the City of Hue
Marines fought with courage
And always won the day

On thing in common
Every woman and man
Had courage in their hearts
And they were able to stand

Against forces outnumbered
And perils untold
To press ever onward
Or at minimum — to hold

It's not whether fear
Is still part of the scrum
It's whether that fear
We've now overcome

Closing out with a saying
From the late John Wayne
Courage is being afraid
And saddling up anyway

My child, I'm still afraid

Dear recruit, I'm still afraid
About what may transpire
My worries for you
Produced thoughts rather dire

I know I shouldn't
Worry or dread
But my emotions run high
As I lie here in bed

My baby is struggling
On an island far away
Learning and growing
And my mind goes astray

Swimming and running
Karate chops, too
What if an injury
Happens to you?

I cannot help worrying
My face is all flushed
Emotional whirlwind
And my heart is now crushed

But no news is good news
I keep telling myself
As I look at your picture
Sitting on the shelf

The phone doesn't ring
That I understand
But a letter would steady
My quivering hand

So I pray once again
Dear God, on my knees
Bless my recruit
Keep them safe, if You please

A quick check online
To set my heart right
With my support family
Before saying good night

Tomorrow a letter
My fears would decrease
But for now I must rest
And put my heart at peace

One more prayer as I look out
At the starry sky up above
Open my heart to my recruit
And send out all my love

To be a statue

To be a statue
Standing still and tall
Is part of our training
In our squad bay hall

Don't look around
Keep your eyes straight ahead
Quiet your mind
Put aside all your dread

Go over your general orders
Recite them line by line
But don't use your voice
Just speak them in your mind

Recall all your training
You took in the classes
Don't twitch your nose
Don't adjust your glasses

I can't really tell
If the DI is standing behind
Or if he's just playing
Another game with my mind

But to stand tall and strong
It's what Marines do
When they're not making trouble
For an enemy or two

But why stand so still
And why stand so long?
It seems counterproductive
Sometimes it feels wrong

But I remember seeing Marines
Standing guard in various places
Protecting their post
No expression on their faces

Whether at an embassy
Or a base gated and fenced
Where Marines are standing guard
No one dares go against

So this discipline now
We all have to learn
If the title of Marine
We now wish to earn

Theres a buzzing sensation
I continue to hear
And now there's a sand flea
Parked on my ear

So pray for me, Mom
I can't move an inch
I dare not scratch
And I better not flinch

How do you do it?

How can you stand still
For what seems like an hour?
When I asked the same thing
Your face would turn sour

When you were at home
You would twiddle and fidget
You couldn't sit still
For even two minutes

But now the secret
I think I discover
Maybe I should have
Earned a Smokey Bear cover

Of course I'm only joking
No intention to insult
I'm proud to know you're growing
Into a responsible adult

Still I can't help wondering
How so long you can stand
Not moving or even twitching
As the bugs come out of the sand

You'd think they'd let you scratch
Once a day at the very least
'Fresh recruits!' Say the sand fleas
As they fly to start a feast

I guess it's all part
Of your disciplinary training
Since you're not allowed
I'll be the one complaining

So I'll sigh off for now
Train hard and sleep tight
Got to end with a joke
Don't let the sand fleas bite

Bayonet Course

This morning we learned
How to use a new threat
At the ends of our rifles
Are fixed bayonets

Long, sharp knives
Sticking out past the muzzle
And a team of three
Trods a course like a puzzle

Through a large pipe
And under a wall
Stab at the tire
Then get down and crawl

Screaming and shouting
And a fair bit of chanting
'Marine Corps! Marine Corps!'
Out of breath, started panting

The DI shouts
To move us along
To the next fighting section
No time, just be strong

Courses like this
Do more than simulate
In a really tough fight
Our training guides our fate

So go for the gusto
Struggle, fight, and strive
What we learn here now
May likely save lives

Finally finished
Worn out, voices hoarse
But we all did well
In the bayonet course

Team Week

This week seemed easier
In a different sort of way
It's called Team Week
Certainly a lower stress day

They divvied us up
Into squads of nine
And sent us various places
To keep our base looking fine

Raking up the leaves
Polishing the brass
Making certain we pick up
Every single piece of trash

With my team every sidewalk
Got a thorough good sweeping
Tonight at lights out
We won't have trouble sleeping

One thing I noticed
Lots of cars driving around
Some held out their cameras
But I looked to the ground

Didn't want to make it obvious
Or get anyone in trouble
Get caught and we'll be busy
Turning rocks into rubble

So I didn't look up
While I picked up some clutter
Yet showed some of my face
To the clicking camera shutter

Maybe, just maybe
My face you will see
So you'll know I'm ok
Working beneath a tree

This week is a nice break
From the daily training grind
Hopefully on Facebook
Your recruit you will find

Under the tree

I found him! I saw her!
My heart is filled with glee!
I saw my recruit
Raking under a tree

Team Week on the schedule
Easier time, but not free
But good to see my recruit
Working under a tree

Someone on Family Day
Did a favor for me
Taking tons of pictures
Of recruits by a tree

He's camera shy
But the face I could see
Was definitely my son
Grabbing sticks by the tree

The recruiter was right
With one guarantee
He's looking much stronger
Cleaning up by the tree

So grateful for the mother
Taking two pix — or three
I'm so happy to notice
My recruit at the tree

So when my turn comes
And we bring the family
I'll be certain to take pictures
Of recruits by the tree

Picture Day

One of our tasks
During Team Week
Was to get portraits taken
As our curiosity they pique

How do they snap
So many photos of recruits
When we're only wearing cammies
And our heavy boots?

The portraits are in our Blues
Not in camouflage green
We haven't even been fitted
And we are not yet Marines

So into the studio
One by one we do file
And the tell us distinctly
That we are not to smile

A few volunteers
A DI did assign
Help the rest of the platoon
Who were standing in line

Some with white covers
You call them 'hats'
Others with, wait a minute
What in the world is that?

A strange looking coat
That fastens in the back
With sleeves to the elbows
Several on a rack

They're the uniforms we would wear
But only for a short time
Stand still, snap the pic
Now get back in line

Take off the cover
And the strange looking coat
Took less time for pictures
Than to write this short note

But somehow it'll simulate
Us wearing Dress Blues
I'll be sure to order prints
With frames you can use

And while I'm among hundreds
No different from the rest
You, my dear mother
Deserve only the best

So I'm ordering something extra
A little surprise
A brooch with my portrait
To show everyone's eyes

Because while miles are between us
Our bond will not sever
You're my Mother, and I love you
For ever and ever

New uniforms

It's getting closer, I can feel it
Just how do I know?
We're measuring for service uniforms
But this process is slow

It's not like getting cammies
That we just tighten with a belt
These are properly measured
Well tailored, not just 'felt'

To get it right, they take their time
Top quality, no trashing
Making our service uniforms sharp
Will cause us to look dashing

First the greens, then the blues
Accessories galore
Belts and buckles, tie clips and buttons
And there's still plenty more

Into a sea bag
Most of it will go
Tailored coats and trousers
Into bins in a row

Other than inspections
This stuff will stay stored
Until after the crucible
When we have Marines on board

Can't contain the excitement
But I need to tamp it down
Still a long way to go
To earn the title renowned

Now I see why the DIs
Their high standards abide
It's not just example
It's more about pride

'Too many Marines
Fought both day and night
To give you a chance

To give you the right'

'So when it's your turn
To wear it side by side
With other Marines
You wear it with pride!'

ZZ Top was right
I'll be as sharp as I can
'Cuz every girl's crazy
About a sharp-dressed man!'

Another test

Closing out Team Week
With yet another test
Rest assured, Dear Mom
We are doing our best

Every day we prepare
Most things memorized
So no questions should come
To us as surprise

We've practiced and studied
Every spare moment's time
And memorized some things
By putting them to rhyme

This test is written
Multiple choice
Just fill in the answer
And keep quiet your voice

You taught me quite well, Mom
I'm fully prepared
If everyone stays focused
No one should be scared

So many areas
We all have to juggle
Physical and mental
Are part of the struggle

I've no doubt we all passed
We prepared as a team
Just another obstacle to overcome
As we live out our dream

Third hike

Our third hike was today
This time six miles
Wasn't too bad
Just one of many trials

But after this hike
Our barracks did change
For the next two weeks
We're at the rifle range

Another hike finished
As that Title we earn
Didn't know this island
Had so many turns

As we approach
The wide open field
We see for the first time
With our eyes unpeeled

'This is your new home now
Take in an eyeful
First thing Monday morning
You learn more about your rifle!'

Also on Monday
We meet a new set of Marines
Marksmanship Instructors
Who aren't quite as mean

More soft spoken
Though they wear a Smokey Bear
To help us hit our targets
Away from the DIs glare

This is the one thing
We all must qualify
So pray that we learn
And keep a steady hand and eye

Now that we're here
It's time to unpack
And write a quick letter

Before hitting the rack

Tomorrow is Sunday
All this pressure we have to grapple
So I'll be praying extra hard
When we get to the Chapel

Signing off now
Got to clean off by boots
Coming next week
We learn how to shoot

Another Sunday down

Another Sunday down
This time, week five
Got another letter
And hoping you thrive

Everyone here in town
Is asking 'how's your recruit?'
And hoping your training
Is bearing good fruit

I've asked them to join me
Every Wednesday in prayer
As we gather at church
Where we lift up our care

We've been taught to ask
The Lord for our need
I just hope I'm not asking
Too much some speed

To the time I have to wait
Until I hug you again
But the trials of waiting
Have me under a strain

'Cast your cares on Him
For He careth for you'
That old-time song
Lifts me out of the blues

Now that Church is over
Off to get some lunch
They won't let me eat alone
What a caring, loving bunch

So focus and stay strong
Don't you worry about me
I'm well taken care of
If I stay on my knees

Safety first

The Monday of Grass Week
Is nothing mysterious
It's all about safety
And of this they are most serious

A special block in our rifle
That is easily eyed
So everyone knows
There's no round inside

Our rifles remain unloaded
Until we are ready to shoot
They don't want accidents
To happen to any recruit

Range rules and briefings
And a few safety signs
Before we learn positions
We need safety on our minds

At this point, we get it
The picture is crystal clear
Don't do anything stupid
If we want to get out of here

Lives are at stake
Every day, every minute
Learn the rules of the range
If you want to stay in it

Thankfully all are listening
Full attention we now give
We want to do it right
We all want to live

Even those with experience
With their fathers' shotguns
Had eyes and ears open
From the moment we'd begun

So, dear Mom, don't you worry
We've got this as well
Safety is first
So let your fears now dispel

Final Drill

It comes down to this
Culmination of our skill
Today we compete
With all platoons in Final Drill

Before learning positions
And marksmanship instruction
We compete for the top spot
Give our all, no deduction

Uniforms pressed
Boots and rifles clean
Now another step closer
To becoming a Marine

Our Senior DI
Whom we've come to respect
Draws his sword, shouts 'FALL IN!'
And he begins to direct

Every step, every move
Every single command
Is deliberate and sharp
Not one quivering hand

Time between major movements
Paused for evaluation
While the Drill Masters inspect
And grade the situation

Eyes front, ears open
And forward we move
We practiced so long
And we've found our full groove

Before we all started
Some nerves were a wreck
Knowing thousands of Marines
Marched across this parade deck

But once underway
We had started out right
As close to perfection
As we practiced last night

Once we had finished
We sit in the stands to watch the others
The DI said, 'Not bad
But don't write home to your mothers.'

That may seem like an insult
To you and to me
But what he meant was praise
To the highest degree

We're about halfway done
And they won't say it aloud
But from the look on their faces
Our DIs seem quite proud

Rest well, Marine

Those yellow footprints
On which you stood
Just after you left
Our quiet neighborhood

Showed you wanted
A little bit more
Than ordinary life
Which would become a bore

Your DIs shouted
Every command
The Recruits replied
Aye Aye Sir — or Ma'am

PT, knowledge
And close order drill
Your time on the island
Was more than just 'kill'

Until finally the Crucible
Your company did start
It wasn't just physical
It required lots of heart

And now that you're home
You plop in my chair
Ten days of leave
With little time to spare

Relax, my Marine
Rest well, and sleep tight
Don't worry at all
I have fire watch tonight

57013306R00093

Made in the USA
Columbia, SC
04 May 2019